TEENAGE MUTANT NINJA TURTLES

MY ADVENTURES WITH THE TURTLES

This book was especially w
Luke Thomson
with love from
Aunt Nettie & Uncle Andy

D0889059

Adapted by Wendy Elks

ISBN 978-1-875676-55-2

A long time ago, a man named Hamato Yoshi bought four turtles at a pet store. Out on the street, Hamato saw a man walking in a strange way, almost like a robot.

Hamato decided to follow him.

In an alleyway, a rat ran up Hamato's leg. The strange man saw Hamato and threw a canister at him—SMASH! The canister broke, splashing green goo all over Hamato, the turtles and the rat.

The goo caused a chemical reaction. The turtles grew to human size, and Hamato grew fur and a tail. Hamato had become a human rat, and the turtles were mutants! Hamato Yoshi became Splinter.

For fifteen years, he and the Turtles lived together in the sewer.

Meanwhile, not too far away in Broomfield, a boy named Luke was growing up.

In the sewer of the city, the Turtles were growing up, too. They called Splinter 'Sensei' which means 'teacher'. Splinter was teaching the Turtles how to be ninjas. They were the Teenage Mutant Ninja Turtles!

Leonardo was brave.

Michelangelo liked to have fun.

Donatello was smart and loved gadgets.

Raphael was tough.

One day, Luke, Grady, Dad and Mom went to the City. It was September 7th, Luke's birthday.

It was also the Turtles' fifteenth birthday, and they wanted to see the City. The Turtles had never been above ground. Splinter thought that people would be afraid of them.

Splinter wasn't sure that the Turtles were ready, but in the end he let them go. "Don't let anyone see you," he warned.

The Turtles cheered.

At that very moment, Luke, Grady, Dad and Mom were walking along the street, right above them!

The Turtles peeked out of a manhole and saw the street for the first time. It was dark and spooky.

"It's so beautiful," Michelangelo exclaimed.

Luke, Grady, Dad and Mom stared in surprise at the strange looking creatures that appeared before them. The Turtles stared back.

"We're not supposed to be seen by anyone," Leonardo said. "Can you keep a secret, and not tell anyone you saw us?"

"Yes," replied Luke. "We'll be your friends."

As they walked down the street together, Luke, Grady, Dad and Mom explained about the items in the shop windows that the Turtles had never seen before.

The city was filled with incredible surprises. There were bright lights and tall buildings. Noisy cars sped up and down the streets... vroom, vroom!

"It's great up here!" said Michelangelo.

"Yeah!" agreed Donatello. He swung his bo staff above his head with excitement. Whoosh!

The best surprise for the Turtles was...pizza!

"I never thought I'd taste anything better than worms and algae," said Raphael. "This is amazing!"

It was a special treat for Luke, too, because it was his birthday.

"Happy birthday, Luke!" the Turtles sang together.

Soon it was time to go and as they headed back to the sewer, they saw a girl walking with her dad. Her name was April.

"She's the most beautiful girl I've ever seen," Donatello said.

"She's the only girl you've ever seen!" Raphael replied.

A white van came driving quickly along the road. Suddenly the van screeched to a stop. Strangers jumped out and grabbed April and her dad!

The Turtles rushed to help, followed by Luke, Grady, Dad and Mom. The Turtles kept bumping into each other. Leonardo hit Raphael and Michelangelo tripped over Donatello. While the Turtles were tangled up, the strangers escaped with April and her dad.

One bad guy was left behind and Michelangelo fought him.
He was very strong, but Michelangelo used all the ninja skills
Splinter had taught him.

Smash! Pow!

Luke, Grady, Dad and Mom stood by, ready to help if they could. It was scary and exciting watching the fight. Luke wanted to jump in and help Michelangelo—they were friends.

"No, Luke," said Leonardo. "It's too dangerous."

Michelangelo won the fight, but then something strange happened. BLOOP! A weird pink blob popped out of the bad guy's chest – he was really a robot with a brain!

The brain scurried away before Michelangelo could show anyone. When he told his brothers about it, they didn't believe him.

"I know I saw it!" said Michelangelo.

Luke bravely spoke up to support his friend. He knew Michelangelo was telling the truth. "I saw it too," he said. "It was pink, and ugly, with green eyes."

"Let's go and see what Splinter thinks about this," said Donatello.

Back in the sewer, the Turtles told Splinter
about the failed rescue attempt.

"I need to train you as a team," Splinter said.
"Next year you can go to the surface again."

But Donatello couldn't wait. He wanted to save April straight away!

Splinter nodded. "Then you will need a leader." He chose Leonardo.

Later, the Turtles returned to the streets. Luke, Grady, Dad and Mom were there, waiting for them. The Turtles wanted to save April and her dad from those horrible bullies, and so did Luke.

Together they tracked down the van that the bad guys had used. Luke, Grady, Dad, Mom and the Turtles hid and waited for the driver to come back.

When he saw the driver coming, Leonardo said, "I have a daring plan." But the other Turtles were already running towards the van!

They chased after the van as it drove away, jumping over rooftops to keep up. Leonardo threw a Throwing Star weapon at the van. It swerved and crashed.

SCREEECH! BANG!

Raphael opened the back of the van. It was full of the same green goo that had turned the Turtles into mutants.

"Keep back, Luke!" shouted Leonardo. "You might turn into a rat, like Splinter."

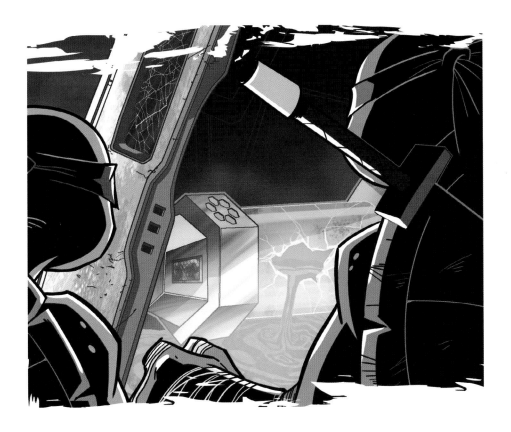

"This is huge," Leonardo said. "These bad guys have something to do with us."

"How is that possible?" Donatello asked.

"Anything is possible for alien robots!" Michelangelo said.

Raphael took a canister of green goo from the van and shoved it in the driver's face.

"This stuff can turn you into a mutant like us," he said. "Tell us what's going on." He tipped the canister a bit.

"Okay!" the driver said. "My name is Snake. Those guys are called the Kraang. They're grabbing scientists. I don't know why."

Snake showed the Turtles the Kraang's hideout.

Raphael wanted to attack right away, but Leonardo wanted to make a plan first. While they were arguing, Snake escaped!

The Turtles, Luke, Grady, Dad and Mom chased Snake over the rooftops and into an alleyway. But he disappeared! Luke nudged Leonardo and pointed. Snake was hiding behind some bins. Leonardo had a plan.

"Oh great, we let him get away," Leonardo said loudly so that Snake could hear him. "Let's drive the van up to the gate at midnight."

Later, the van raced up to the door of the Kraang's hideout. Snake and the Kraang thought it was the Turtles. ZAP! They destroyed the van! Green goo splashed everywhere and covered the Snake. But the van was empty. Where were the Turtles?

The Turtles had created the distraction so that they could sneak into the hideout! Luke, Grady, Dad and Mom climbed up the steep walls with them. They crept through the darkness. Luke was a bit scared but he was glad to have Grady, Dad, Mom and the brave Turtles with him.

They discovered that the Kraang were really brain-like aliens that used robots to move around. They wanted April's dad, a famous scientist, to help them with an evil plan.

They found a holding cell – April and her dad were inside!
Donatello tried to pick the lock but it wouldn't open.

Raphael started smashing the door! Just as it was about to
break, the Kraang came back and dragged April and her dad away.

The Turtles, Luke, Grady, Dad and Mom started to chase the Kraang, but Snake blocked their path. Now Snake was huge! He was covered in leaves and thorns. The green goo had mutated him!

"It's Snake, but he's a giant weed!" Leonardo said.

"He's Snakeweed!" Michelangelo yelled.

The Turtles tried to fight past Snakeweed. Luke, Grady, Dad and Mom fought hard too.

Every time they sliced off one of his branches, it grew straight back.

"No fair!" Donatello said.

Some of the Kraang forced April and her dad into a helicopter. Luke tried to grab the running robots, but they were too slippery. What an adventure!

As the helicopter took off, Donatello leaped onto one of its landing skids to stop them. The helicopter spun and rocked and April fell out!

Donatello saved April, but the Kraang flew away with her dad.

The rest of the Kraang turned back towards their attackers who were now stuck between Snakeweed and the Kraang!

Suddenly, Leonardo had an idea. He ran to the hideout's power generator. The Kraang turned their blasters towards him and fired, but Leonardo jumped aside at the last second.

KABLAAM! The Kraang's blasters blew up the generator and destroyed the hideout!

Luckily the Turtles, April, Luke, Grady, Dad and Mom were able to escape from the blast.

That was enough excitement for now!

It was time for Luke, Grady, Dad and Mom to go home to Broomfield. They said goodbye to the Turtles and April and promised to keep their secret safe, and maybe even come back to see them some day!

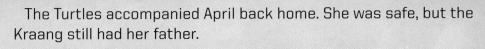

The Turtles accompanied April back home. She was safe, but the Kraang still had her father.

"We won't rest until we find him," Donatello said.

"We?" asked April. "This isn't your fight."

"It is now," said Donatello. "Because we are a team!"

   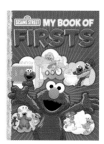 

This personalized My Adventures with the Turtles book was especially created for Luke Thomson of 1207 Loch Ness Ave., Broomfield, with love from Aunt Nettie & Uncle Andy.

1093 000985 0001 01 DS 0016